Dear Parent:
Your child's love of reading starts here!

Every child learns to read in a different way and at his or her own speed. Some go back and forth between reading levels and read favorite books again and again. Others read through each level in order. You can help your young reader improve and become more confident by encouraging his or her own interests and abilities. From books your child reads with you to the first books he or she reads alone, there are I Can Read Books for every stage of reading:

SHARED READING
Basic language, word repetition, and whimsical illustrations, ideal for sharing with your emergent reader

BEGINNING READING
Short sentences, familiar words, and simple concepts for children eager to read on their own

READING WITH HELP
Engaging stories, longer sentences, and language play for developing readers

READING ALONE
Complex plots, challenging vocabulary, and high-interest topics for the independent reader

ADVANCED READING
Short paragraphs, chapters, and exciting themes for the perfect bridge to chapter books

I Can Read Books have introduced children to the joy of reading since 1957. Featuring award-winning authors and illustrators and a fabulous cast of beloved characters, I Can Read Books set the standard for beginning readers.

A lifetime of discovery begins with the magical words **"I Can Read!"**

Visit www.icanread.com for information
on enriching your child's reading experience.

Fancy NANCY

The 100th Day of School

by Jane O'Connor

cover illustration by Robin Preiss Glasser

interior illustrations by Ted Enik

HARPER

An Imprint of HarperCollinsPublishers

For Katie Bellas,
who is 100% fun
to work with
—J.O'C.

For Tamar Mays:
for today and
tamara
—R.P.G.

For E.C.
Astute and amusing,
then "presto!" a Muse
—T.E.

HarperCollins® and I Can Read Book® are trademarks of HarperCollins Publishers.

Fancy Nancy: The 100th Day of School
Text copyright © 2009 by Jane O'Connor Illustrations copyright © 2009 by Robin Preiss Glasser All rights reserved. Manufactured in the United States of America. No part of this book may be used or reproduced in any manner whatsoever without written permission except in the case of brief quotations embodied in critical articles and reviews. For information address HarperCollins Children's Books, a division of HarperCollins Publishers, 10 East 53rd Street, New York, NY 10022.
www.icanread.com

Library of Congress Cataloging-in-Publication Data
O'Connor, Jane.
  The 100th day of school / by Jane O'Connor ; cover illustration by Robin Preiss Glasser ; interior illustrations by Ted Enik. — 1st ed.
    p. cm. — (Fancy Nancy) (I can read! Level 1)
  Summary: Nancy, who likes to use fancy words, decides to make an homage to her little sister's pet goldfish as her project for the 100th day of school.
  ISBN 978-0-06-170374-4 (pbk.) — ISBN 978-0-06-170375-1 (trade bdg.)
  [1. Hundredth day of school—Fiction. 2. Schools—Fiction. 3. Vocabulary—Fiction.] I. Glasser, Robin Preiss, ill. II. Enik, Ted, ill. III. Title. IV. Title: Hundredth day of school. V. Title: One hundredth day of school.
PZ7.O222Aak 2009
[E]—dc22
2008055607
CIP
AC

10 11 12 13 LP/WOR 10 9 8 7 6 5 4   ❖   First Edition

It is the 97th day of school,

and I have a dilemma.

(That is a BIG problem.)

I do not know what to bring in

for the 100th day.

Bree put 100 feathers on a hat.

It looks so elegant!

(That's a fancy word for pretty.)

Robert is bringing his stamp album.

There are 100 stamps in it.

Yoko's piggy bank has 100 pennies.

The bank is transparent.

(That means you can see inside.)

Lionel made a ball

out of 100 rubber bands.

After school,

I look all around my room.

I have 39 hair clips.

That is not enough.

I have 57 bracelets.

That is not enough.

I have 84 ribbons.

That is not enough.

What am I going to do?

Now it is the 98th day of school.

More kids bring in stuff:

a bag with 100 marbles,

a jar with 100 jelly beans,

a box with 100 crayons.

I tell Ms. Glass my dilemma.

She tells me not to worry.

"You are very imaginative.

That means you are

full of good ideas.

You will think of something."

At home,

I tell Mom my dilemma.

She is making dinner.

"How about a poster

with macaroni?" she says.

I do not want

to hurt Mom's feelings.

Three kids have already

done stuff with macaroni.

Macaroni is not imaginative.

Dad is doing the wash.

Maybe he will have a good idea.

Dad says,

"I bet we have fifty pairs of socks.

That makes one hundred."

I do not want

to hurt Dad's feelings.

But socks are ugly.

I want something imaginative

and fancy.

After dinner,

I try to think some more.

All of a sudden,

I hear my sister crying.

"Look," my sister says.

She points at her fishbowl.

Goldy is her goldfish.

Goldy is not moving.

We bury Goldy in our yard.

Everyone is sad, even Frenchy.

I am so glad that

dogs live a long time.

We put a few pebbles

from Goldy's bowl on top.

I tell my sister,

"We will remember Goldy fondly."

Fondly means with love.

The next day, I write a poem.

Goldy was gold.
For a fish, she was old.
She liked to swim,
So she stayed slim.
You can't Kiss a fish.
But you can miss a fish.

Ms. Glass likes my poem.

She reads it to the class.

"Nancy uses interesting words.

Slim means thin.

Her poem is in verse.

It rhymes."

At home,

it is sad to see the empty fishbowl.

Mom is about to throw out

the pebbles.

Then, all of a sudden,

I get an idea that is imaginative.

"Stop!" I say.

I wash and dry all the pebbles.

They are so pretty.

I count them.

Yes! There are 104!

I get my markers.

I get a huge piece of paper.

Huge is even bigger than big.

I will make a poster.

I spell out Goldy's name
in glitter.

I draw a picture of Goldy
in her bowl.

Then I glue on the pebbles.

I let my sister help.

I write on the poster,

"There are 100 pebbles

in the fishbowl."

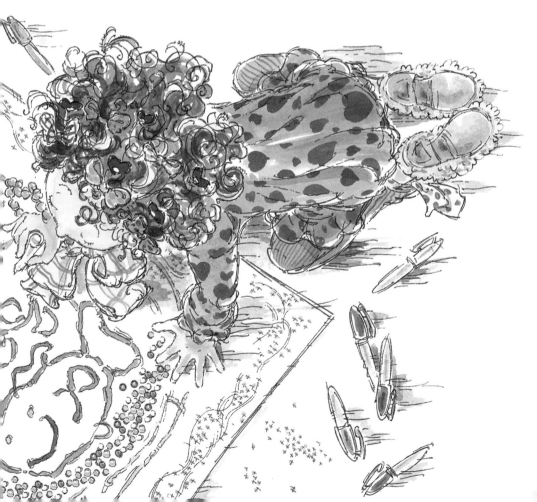

Today is the 100th day of school.

I bring in my poster.

I made it just in time!

Ms. Glass brings in something too.

It's a cart with 100 books.

She will read them all to us

before school ends in June.

Ms. Glass is so imaginative!

Fancy Nancy's Fancy Words

These are the fancy words in this book:

Dilemma—a big problem

Elegant—pretty

Fondly—with love

Huge—even bigger than big

Imaginative—full of good ideas

Slim—thin

Transparent—see-through

Verse—a poem that rhymes